The Elegant Eleanor

BY

Jean Poindexter Colby

WITH ILLUSTRATIONS BY

Marie C. Nichols

HASTINGS HOUSE, PUBLISHERS, NEW YORK

To my son Peter

Published simultaneously in Canada
by S. J. Reginald Saunders, Publishers, Toronto 2B.

Library of Congress Catalog Card Number: 58-8279

Printed in the United States of America

ELEANOR was a very fancy-looking cat. She somehow looked smart the way a person looks who is very neatly dressed. She was all black except for four white feet and the front two were double, with six toes each. They were so big she almost had to walk around them. She had white whiskers and white hairs coming out of her black ears, but best of all she had a white mustache, which made her look as if she had always just finished drinking milk.

She came to the Bigelows' house with her brother Lancelot who looked just like her except he didn't have any white mustache. They were always together—they slept together,

ate together, and played together. For that reason Mr. Bigelow first named them Lancelot and Elaine after two lovers in an old, old poem. But the Bigelow children didn't like Elaine and kept calling her Eleanor, so finally everybody did.

One day, however, Lancelot wandered out of the yard quite far from home and a man came along who thought he, too, was a fancy-looking cat. So, not knowing he belonged to any one, he scooped him up and took him home. Eleanor never saw her brother again even though she called and called him and so did the Bigelows.

Without Lancelot, Eleanor was very lonely. She even tried to make friends with Gerty, the Bigelows' collie dog. That was a foolish thing to do because Gerty hated cats. Ever since they arrived, she had watched Eleanor and Lancelot with eyes half-closed, thinking what fun it would be to catch them.

One day the cats had wandered into her part of the yard and she had trembled all over with desire to chase them. Yet she was worried. One cat she could handle. But two? What would Lancelot do while she went after Eleanor? Or vice versa?

So Gerty was delighted when Lancelot went away. And she was exultant the next afternoon when she saw Eleanor walk slowly down the drive toward her. She planned to wait until the young cat was only a few feet away and then pounce on her. But when there was still a good ten feet between them, she couldn't resist the chance to catch cat any longer.

"Woof, wo-o-o-of," Gerty was a collie and had a terribly loud bark. Except for this bark, she might have caught Eleanor. But the noise scared the cat into action. With three tremendous jumps, which were very big for such a small animal, she was up a tree and safe.

Gerty sat at the base of the tree and howled until the Bigelows called her in.

Eleanor stayed up in the tree until she got very hungry. Then she eased her way down, backward, with much scrabbling, since this was her first tree climbing and she wasn't very good at it.

Gerty watched her from a window and licked her chops.

The next time Gerty and Eleanor were outside, Gerty didn't even pretend to wait. She just flew at the cat. But Eleanor made the same tree safely and looked calmly down with her great big yellow eyes at the dog, howling and rushing around beneath her.

The Bigelow children were worried and so was Mrs. Bigelow, although she didn't admit it.

"We can't keep Gerty in just because we have a cat. After all, we got the cats to get rid of mice and Gerty is here to guard the house. So they will just have to do their jobs and learn to live peacefully together."

"By that time there won't be any Eleanor," said Donny, who was eight.

"No Eleanor," echoed Linda, who was five.

When Eleanor came down from the tree that time, she did it very gracefully and well. She landed on her feet and even gave her long tail a little hike, as if saying, "Pooh to you, Gerty."

And the very next day she seemed purposely to tease Gerty into chasing her. Gerty was lying in the sun, tired out from a hard run with Mr. Bigelow. But she couldn't bear to smell cat so close. Up she sprang, and away they went. This time Eleanor chose a tree farther away and it seemed as if Gerty would surely get at least a piece of her tail, but the cat made the tree all right.

Instead of climbing way up to a branch, however, she stopped after a few feet and looked down at Gerty, racing around below her. They glared at each other for a few minutes while the Bigelow children held their breaths as they watched from the kitchen door.

Suddenly Eleanor let go and dropped to the ground. Gerty doubled up for the final spring but she never made it, for Eleanor had brought her back up high, her tail was swelled to mammoth proportions, and she was spitting hard, showing some very long, sharp teeth.

Gerty skidded to a stop. What was this wild thing ahead? Surely not an easy opponent and probably not worthy of notice.

So the dog carefully looked up at the sky as if wondering about the weather, and turned to walk off. She tried to act as if she didn't care, but when she settled down in the sun again, with her head on her paws, one eye stayed right on Eleanor. As for Eleanor, the air seemed to go out of her tail. She stopped spitting and began to wash one paw as if that had been her only desire all day.

Inside the house, the air seemed to go out of the young Bigelows, too. "Gee, Mother, that was close!" sighed Donny. "How did Eleanor ever dare to do that?"

"Yes, Mother, how did she dare to do that?" asked Linda. "She is so much littler than Gerty."

"Courage doesn't come in sizes," said Mother. "Little people can be just as brave as big people."

"Eleanor is very brave," remarked Donny, "even though she is very little. Braver than I would have been."

"I'm very brave," announced Linda. "I'm braver than even Eleanor."

"Don't boast," said Donny. "Was Eleanor really brave, Mother?"

"I guess she knew she had to stand up to Gerty in order to live here," answered Mother. "Animals seem to figure things out much the way we do sometimes."

The next morning Eleanor had her breakfast of canned mackerel and milk and Gerty had her breakfast of hamburger and egg, and they watched each other across the kitchen while they ate.

"Mother," said Donny, who was finishing his shredded wheat, "Gerty is figuring things out just like a person. Did you see the way she looked at Eleanor? I think there is going to be more war."

"More war," quoted Linda, hammering on the table gleefully with her spoon. "I want more war."

"There'll be war if you don't stop doing that," said her Mother, but they all looked fearfully out of the window because Eleanor had been let out the front door and Gerty out the back, and they weren't very far apart.

Sure enough, Gerty appeared around the corner of the house, walking with very stiff legs and with the hair up along her back. She eyed Eleanor, who was sitting in the driveway, carefully washing her paws and then scraping them over her ears.

She seemed not to be watching Gerty but when the dog rushed at her, quick as a flash she drew herself up in fighting position and began to spit.

Gerty tore right at her, opened her jaws—and then flashed on by, chasing some made-up enemy.

"Oh, Mother, how funny!" cried Donny. "At the last minute she didn't dare bite her!"

"It looked like that," chuckled Mrs. Bigelow, "but perhaps Gerty decided at the last minute it wasn't smart to be brave this time."

"You mean it's like when those big boys picked on me at school? It would have been silly for me to try to fight them?" asked Donny.

"Exactly," answered Mrs. Bigelow. "It was much better to talk it over with them as you did. Now you're friends instead of enemies."

"Sure," agreed Donny, "but those cookies and chocolate milk you gave us certainly helped!"

"If I almost had a fight with a girl, could we have cookies and chocolate milk?" asked Linda.

Everybody laughed until even Linda joined in.

Gerty's war with Eleanor seemed to be over but she would not be friendly. To the children it seemed as if the little cat took needless chances when she rubbed up against the dog and, one night, even curled up against her in front of the fireplace.

Gerty simply moved away, looking very disdainful. This Gerty could do very well. She looked down her long nose like a proud queen-dog paying no attention to an unruly subject.

So Eleanor was still lonely. Gerty would have nothing to do with her but she would not allow other cats on the place either. And as Eleanor got older, she had many admirers in the neighborhood cat world. Many big tomcats thought she was a very fancy-looking cat with her white double paws, white whiskers, and cute white mustache. When Gerty would go in for her supper, several of them would come to call. Three of them were especially enthusiastic: a big tiger cat with a very fierce expression; a handsome all-black Persian tom, and a rugged gray cat with a white chest and many marks of battle.

At first, when Gerty chased them, they flew up the drive and out the gates but soon they began to stand their ground. And when they did that, Gerty would whiz on by as she had that day with Eleanor, making believe she was chasing a squirrel in the distance.

"Mother, I think Gerty *pretends* she is brave sometimes," Donny commented one day. "You don't suppose she is really a coward, do you?"

"No," replied Mother, "but she certainly shows off . . . just the way children or even grown-ups do sometimes."

"I remember showing off one time when Daddy brought me a cowboy suit and I thought I was so much I ran right into a tree and hurt myself." Donny rubbed his nose at the memory.

"I remember that too!" his mother laughed.

"I never show off," spoke up Linda. "Never."

Donny looked at her in disgust and went outside.

When Eleanor was nine or ten months old, Mr. Bigelow said, "I thought we got this cat to catch the mice? Certainly Gerty doesn't do anything about them. Personally, I think she *plays* with them at night."

"Dogs aren't supposed to catch mice," defended Donny.

"And you tell us we're supposed to do what we're supposed to do," added Linda gravely. "I always do."

"Is that so?" asked her father with one eyebrow cocked in her direction. "Well, anyway, Eleanor is supposed to catch mice. Start her to work today. The mice have nibbled a hole in the wall down cellar. And they've chewed the leather cover on my ax."

"I guess Eleanor will have to sleep down cellar then," said Mrs. Bigelow.

"With Gerty?" asked Donny, horrified. "She'll be in little pieces tomorrow."

"I'm betting on Eleanor," answered Mr. Bigelow, and left for his office.

The next morning Donny got up very early and tiptoed to the cellar door. Just as he feared, Gerty came bounding out but there was no sign of Eleanor. Sadly he crept downstairs, his heart beating double time.

First, he looked in the nice bed he had made for the cat in the laundry. He had padded a box with his favorite old sweater which his mother had been very glad to get rid of.

There was no sign of Eleanor in her box.

He looked behind the washing machine and under the work bench. No cat.

Finally, he screwed up his courage and pushed wide open the door to the big, dark part of the cellar where he secretly hated to go. It was piled with firewood and had an old heap of coal in one corner and it smelled damp and gloomy. Furthermore, he couldn't reach the light and he had to feel his way forward through what seemed like a maze of cobwebs.

"Eleanor. Elly, Elly," he called.

No answer.

He called again, and he thought he heard something off in one corner. He felt his way forward some more when there was a sharp squeak and a log of firewood rattled down and fell on the floor with a clunk. Then there was a softer thud, and Donny felt something warm brush against his leg.

It was Eleanor! Proudly she led the way out of the cellar but she didn't talk the way she usually did when she walked in front of Donny. And when both of them reached the laundry he saw why. Hanging from her mouth was a fat mouse!

He tried to take it away from her but she held on tight and trotted ahead of him up the stairs into the kitchen. There were Mrs. Bigelow and Linda.

"O-o-o-h, the poor mousie!" screamed Linda.

"There, dear" Mrs. Bigelow tried to soothe her. "We have to get rid of them before they do any more damage. Perhaps they'll go away now that one of them has been caught."

"O-o-o-h, take it out of her mouth before she eats it!" cried Linda, still very much unsoothed.

But Eleanor would not give up her prey. When they touched it, she growled and sprang up on the sink, right in the middle of eggs Mrs. Bigelow had opened to scramble for breakfast.

"Get down, Eleanor!" shouted Mrs. Bigelow, excited herself now. "You know you aren't supposed to get up there."

Eleanor, her yellow eyes flashing and the mouse still drooping from her mouth, dodged this way and that as Mrs. Bigelow went after her with a dishcloth and Donny with a mixing spoon.

Suddenly into the room came Mr. Bigelow, morning paper in hand.

"What is this uproar?" he shouted over everyone else. "Who is being murdered?"

"A mouse," answered Linda, tearfully and truthfully.

"NO! Where?" asked Mr. Bigelow, delighted.

"In Eleanor's mouth" Donny pointed it out "but you can't get it. She won't let you."

The boy was wrong. Eleanor, as soon as she saw Mr. Bigelow, jumped down from the top of the icebox, her last landing place, and walked slowly up to him. Carefully she laid the mouse down at his feet and started her loud cat-talk. Then she looked up at him as if to say, "How do you like that?"

"There, Daddy!" crowed Linda. "She knew you were the one who wanted the mice caught. She's done what she's supposed to, hasn't she? She's smart, like me. Pat her or something."

"I certainly will," said Mr. Bigelow, and he did. "Eleanor, you are a smart cat. Good for you. You got your orders and you carried them out beautifully. You have set an excellent example." Whereupon he gave Donny a long look. "I had to get the paper off the front porch again this morning. Isn't that your job?"

"Oh-oh," said Donny. "I mean, yes, sir. I guess I ought to do what I'm supposed to, too."

"I always do," echoed Linda. "I was just about to go and brush my teeth before anybody told me to. But let's have a mouse funeral after breakfast, Donny."

Mr. Bigelow picked up the mouse by the tail and went into the library to look for a cigar box that would make a proper final resting place for Eleanor's first catch.

In a few weeks it was obvious by her roundness that Eleanor was going to have kittens. Donny and Linda couldn't wait but Mr. Bigelow said he could wait very nicely.

"The elegant Eleanor has been wooed and won," he said. "Now we will have to deal with a dozen or so kittens. Nature is incorrigible."

"What does incorrigible mean, Daddy?" asked Donny.

"It sounds bad," said Linda.

"It means refusing to be improved," answered Mr. Bigelow.

"Like Grandmother Bigelow?" asked Linda.

"NO!" shouted Daddy, and then he laughed. "I guess I *did* say she wouldn't take anybody's advice the last time we visited her, didn't I? No, she's not incorrigible; just set in her ways."

"I like her," said Linda stoutly. "When I'm grown up I'm going to be set in my ways."

Daddy laughed and hoisted her up on his shoulder. "Sometimes I wonder if you're not like your grandmother already," he said as they all walked in to dinner. "My main worry is what are we going to name the kittens and what is Gerty going to do with them?"

"Oh-o-o," shuddered Linda. "I can't bear to think. The kittens won't be big enough to figure Gerty out and they won't be brave as I am."

"Oh, Linda," groaned Donny. "You're terrible."

"I'm not," insisted Linda. "I'm brave."

Soon Eleanor started prowling from room to room in the house. The whole family followed the little cat around as she went "apartment hunting" as Mr. Bigelow called it. She investigated the back of the china closet and clawed a green bag with silver in it. She walked in and around the guns in

Mr. Bigelow's closet until one fell down and she flew out of there as if she had been shot. The cleaning closet seemed a favorite for a while and Mrs. Bigelow left a pile of rags on the floor there, hopefully. But toward the end it was obvious that the cat preferred a storage-room closet where Mrs. Bigelow hung her old evening dresses. Eleanor kept trying to claw one down off its hanger until Mrs. Bigelow finally doubled up an old one and shoved it back in the corner.

"There," she said, "that was my senior prom dress. I should have thrown it away years ago. It will now serve one final good use."

And Eleanor seemed to agree with her, for she stretched out on the red velvet with obvious delight and her black and whiteness looked very handsome against the bright color.

So did the little kittens the next morning. There were four: a tiny tiger with four white feet and double paws; a black number like Eleanor with just half a white mustache; a big all gray one, and a mixed up one of different colors—a real calico cat.

Donny and Linda thought they were beautiful.

"They *are* beautiful," agreed Mrs. Bigelow, "partly because you have taken such good care of Eleanor.

"Does Eleanor have lovely fur because we give her lots of cat food and milk and liver?" Donny asked.

"I'm the one who gives her milk and cat food and liver," interrupted Linda. "I take good care of Eleanor."

A hot argument was stopped by the sudden appearance of Gerty at the "bedside" of the kittens.

"Oh, Mother," cried Linda in alarm, beginning to scoop up the kittens. "Help! Gerty will eat them up!"

Mrs. Bigelow made no move to help nor did Donny after one look at his mother. As Gerty approached, the smell of cat made her ears prick up and her head thrust forward.

Eleanor, however, saw the dog coming. Boldly she flashed out in front of her, spitting and clawing as she went. Gerty beat a hasty retreat, and the Bigelow family relaxed again. Eleanor was not happy, though, until Linda had put down the two kittens she held and every one of them was back in the nest. Then Eleanor licked them hard, rolling them from side to side, and finally curling up beside them, purring like a noisy machine.

"My, she looks proud, doesn't she?" said Donny. "She seems to know they are nice kittens."

"Let's leave her with her family and go down and have breakfast," suggested Mrs. Bigelow. And they all tiptoed downstairs.

The kittens grew and were soon scratching their way across the polished floor, trying to stay on their feet. Pearl, the gray one, and Blimp, the tiger, who was very fat and round, were the liveliest. Eleanor had to carry them back to the nest many times from far corners of the house where they had crawled. Once Blimp and Gerty met head-on around a corner and Gerty was as surprised as the tiny kitten. Linda happened to be on hand at the time and screamed with delight when the kitten arched his back, swelled up to tea cup size, and hissed a tiny hiss at the big dog. He even made a swipe at his huge enemy with a paw no bigger than a dime.

"Mother, Mother!" cried Linda. "The kittens are brave, too, just like me and Eleanor. Blimp made war on Gerty and Gerty ran away. The cats are sure to win now there are five of them."

"Maybe so," replied her mother. "But Gerty is a smart dog. You watch her and see what she does next."

"I know what she'll do next. She'll chase them the way she did Eleanor. Gerty loves to chase anything. Then we'll have war. I love war."

Mrs. Bigelow said nothing. Instead, she looked at her small daughter, puzzled.

Poor Gerty, her days of peace seemed to be over. The kittens were all over the house. She couldn't even curl up on her favorite rug without one staggering over to disturb her rest.

When that happened, Gerty would get up with a great sigh and move to another place or another room.

Mr. Bigelow kept tripping over the kittens until one day he said, "We're up to our knees in cats. Four kittens is four too many. I'm sick of finding kitten in my shoes, in my socks, on my pillow. They have to GO!"

Mrs. Bigelow agreed that two, at least, must go, and she was going to call up the Humane Society when Linda began to cry and Donny's face grew longer and longer.

"Couldn't we find nice homes for them?" he asked. "I could ask around at school."

"No," answered Linda before her mother could reply. "I can find a home for the kitties. I know lots of people who would want kitties. I'll go now."

Donny started to say, "I'll help you," but a look from his mother held him back. "She sure thinks she's great," he said when his sister had marched out the door and down the drive.

"I know," soothed his mother, "but she will have to find out for herself what she can do and what she can't do."

"She has to figure things out for herself just like Gerty and Eleanor, you mean?" Donny looked doubtful.

"Yes," answered his mother. "We all have to."

"Well, I sure wish she would hurry," sighed her brother.

In an hour an exhausted Linda dragged her feet up the walk. "Nobody wants kittens," she admitted. "People gave me cookies and apples and candy but they wouldn't take a kitten. They said I was brave, though, to go around asking all by myself. I am very brave, aren't I, Mother?"

"I guess it did take courage," answered her mother, "but you didn't solve our problem."

"Brave," snorted Donny. "I'd call it something else."

The next day at school Donny found two boys who wanted kittens. They ran home and got permission to have them, and then they all went over to Donny's house after school.

The boys had a little trouble choosing, but one finally settled on the calico and the other chose the black and white. They picked them up in their arms and started out of the house with Eleanor following and miaowing worriedly. Gerty followed Eleanor, obviously wondering what was going on when, at the gate, Eleanor started very loud talking. This time her miaowing had a different sound and Gerty pricked up her ears as if she were trying to understand. Suddenly Eleanor ran back toward Gerty, where-

upon the dog lay back her ears and ran snarling at the boys, jumping up on their arms and racing around them. The boys cried out in alarm.

"Goodness, what's happening?" asked Mrs. Bigelow from the front door.

"Mother, call Gerty. I don't think she wants the kittens to go," cried Donny. "Eleanor told her to stop the boys from taking them. She did, Mother, just as plain as day. And Gerty did what Eleanor told her to."

"Well, boys," said Mrs. Bigelow to the frightened children, "why don't you leave the kittens here since Gerty and Eleanor want you to? Mr. Bigelow will bring them around to you tonight after the animals go to bed. Perhaps if Eleanor wakes up and two of her children are gone, she won't feel so badly as seeing them go off with strangers."

"But, Mother, that isn't fair to Gerty and Eleanor," objected Donny. "They stopped the boys from carrying off the kittens and they've earned the right to have them."

"In a way that's true, Donny," Mrs. Bigelow agreed, "but animals have to make the best of what we think is best for them."

"It isn't fair," repeated Donny disgustedly.

"Donny, wait for a few days," his mother asked softly.

"If you can truthfully say that Gerty and Eleanor still miss the kittens, then we'll get them back again."

"That's a deal," said Donny.

"That's a deal," echoed Linda.

"Oh, go fly a kite," answered Donny crossly, and ran up to his room.

That night Mr. Bigelow delivered the kittens to the boys' homes and the next day Eleanor bounded outside as soon as Mrs. Bigelow came down to take in the milk. But instead of running off into the next yard, as she usually did, she stayed around the back door miaowing loudly. She walked in and out of the shrubs in back of the house, talking and talking, and then nervously darting back to the door when she heard it open. Twice she went back to the nest and rolled the two remaining kittens over with her nose as if she were looking for the others and counting those she had.

Gerty, when she was let out, seemed to join in the search. Again and again she put her long nose to the ground and seemed to follow a vague trail down the front steps. Then she would come back to the front porch and flop down on the doormat in disgust.

Donny and Linda watched all this in great distress.

"Eleanor certainly does miss her kittens and so does

Gerty," Donny told his mother. "I think we ought to get them back. You said we could."

"Oh, dear," sighed Mrs. Bigelow, "we seem to have very sensitive animals. When I was a little girl I don't remember our old mother cat bothering like this, and certainly not our collie dog. I guess I was wrong about Eleanor not missing those two we gave away. It's quite pitiful to watch her, isn't it?"

"Pitiful," echoed Linda. "It makes me feel not like breakfast. I'll go get the cats away from the boys. I'm brave. I'd like to do that."

"Wait one more day," urged her mother. "Daddy thinks they will have better homes and get more attention where there is only one cat."

The children agreed reluctantly and Mrs. Bigelow hurried to pack a picnic so they could go to the park and not have to watch Eleanor's maternal distress.

The next day Eleanor had stopped her calling and roaming around but she kept going back to the nest to be sure the last two kittens were safe. It was a lovely day and finally she left them and stretched out on a part of the driveway that had been warmed by the sun. She even rolled back and forth in enjoyment while Gerty watched with apparent approval from another warm spot.

Suddenly, after one especially big stretch and a quick bat at a bug that flew past, Eleanor jumped up and made for the back door that stood open to let in the spring warmth. In a moment or two the children heard a bump, bump, bump on the back stairs and Eleanor appeared with Pearl in her mouth. The kitten was all doubled up, trying to avoid being bruised, but Eleanor held her firmly by the back of the neck, her yellow eyes flashing with determination. Bump, bump, she carried her child down the back steps and plunked her on the warm spot in the driveway. Pearl

promptly uncoiled and tried to scramble away, but Eleanor pulled her back by her neck, growling fiercely. Then she put a big double front paw on her child and looked down sternly, as if to say, "You stay there! Hear?"

The two children, watching from inside, burst out laughing, as did Mrs. Bigelow.

"Look," cried Linda. "Look at Gerty. She looks as if she was laughing, too!" And she did. Gerty's mouth was open and she really looked as if she were laughing.

Soon Eleanor seemed to have impressed Pearl with the fact she must stay in the warm spot, and the kitten curled up with her four tiny feet under her, a gray fur ball on the drive. Then Eleanor disappeared into the house once more and in a minute they could all hear bump, bump, bump again. Out she came with Blimp, who was protesting his first trip more than his sister. He was heavier, too, and Eleanor had to hold her head very high to keep him off the ground.

Finally, she set him down by his sister with what seemed an unnecessarily hard thump. He sprang to his feet and skittered off sideways but Eleanor didn't go after him as she had Pearl. Instead, she stretched out in the sun and blinked her yellow eyes at her offspring. This seemed to be a dinner bell unheard by human ears for both scrambled up to her and began their breakfast. After they had their fill, they curled up beside their mother and went to sleep.

At that, Eleanor turned her head toward Gerty and a long look passed between them. Then Eleanor also closed her eyes and went to sleep.

"Oh, Mother," cried Linda in delight. "She asked Gerty to guard them all just as plain as day, didn't she?"

"She certainly seemed to," said Mrs. Bigelow. "I must say I never expected Gerty to play watchdog to a cat family."

"It's a nice cat family," added Donny, "and I agree with Daddy. It's big enough. It would be hard for Gerty and Eleanor to take care of any more." Linda thought so, too, so they didn't go back for the other kittens.

*　　*

As the spring leaves came out on the trees and bushes, they hid various things on the Bigelow place. One was an

old chicken house that Mr. Bigelow was always going to tear down and never got around to. Beside it, halfway down a little hill, lay a coil of barbed wire the former owners had used to keep skunks and foxes out of the yard.

One day, as the cats lay sunning themselves again, two dogs came running into the yard and made for them. Gerty was on guard, as usual, and she sprang to her feet, every hair bristling.

"Wow-ow-ow-ow-ow," she bellowed, and dashed off the porch after them. One was a large police dog and the other a big mongrel tan animal with a chewed-up head and

ugly eyes. They stopped in surprise in the middle of their charge on the cats, looked at Gerty and then tore off up the hill with the collie in pursuit. Soon they curved down by the old hen house with Gerty about ten feet behind. As they reached the house, Gerty gave a big leap from the top of the hill, trying to make up the distance. Unfortunately she landed right on top of the barbed wire which was now covered by a leafy vine. Howls of pain came from the poor animal, who pulled herself off toward the house, badly injured.

As the two intruders ran away down the drive, the children and their mother hurried out of the house to Gerty. Mrs. Bigelow got to her first and saw that the dog's wounds were more than surface cuts.

"Pull that old blanket off the line," she called to Donny, who turned in his tracks to do his mother's bidding. "I'll hold her," she told Linda, "while you two slide the blanket under her. And watch out. Injured animals sometimes bite even the ones they love."

But Gerty seemed to know she was in good hands. Mrs. Bigelow disappeared in the house for bandages while the two children soothed their pet. A quick call was made to the veterinarian who promised to be on hand when they arrived with the dog. Then Mrs. Bigelow, together with Donny, got Gerty into the car while Linda took the kittens inside to safety.

The veterinarian complimented them all on the dog's care. "Keeping her quiet so she wouldn't lose much blood was very important. And I'm glad to find her so clean. I'll take a few stitches and she'll be all right in a couple of days."

Carefully he put Gerty in a clean cage and then turned to say good-bye to the Bigelow family.

"Don't worry, now," he advised them kindly. "Call me tonight and I'll let you know just how she is. But I'd get rid of that wire if I were you."

Before their car had really come to a stop in the drive, Donny was out and over at the chicken house pulling the vine off the wire.

Mrs. Bigelow said, "*I'll* get rid of that wire after I fix some lunch for us. It's too heavy for you two to move. Just pull the vine off it for now." And she went inside to cook.

But Donny and Linda thought differently. Donny went to the tool-house and got heavy garden gloves for them both. "We don't want to get scratched, too. But let's show Mother we can move this thing."

"How?" asked Linda simply. "It's awful big." Then she added, "Oh, I have an idea. Wait a second." And she ran off to the garage where they stored their toys.

While she was gone, Donny worked away, freeing the wire from the vine and the leaves and stones that had started to bury it over the years. He found an old piece of iron pipe in the chicken house and used it to pry up first one end and then the other. In fact, it was almost free when Linda came running back, trundling their play wagon behind her.

"We can pull it down to the sidewalk on this," she said.

Donny wiped the perspiration from his forehead. "That's a good idea, but how are we going to get it on the cart. It's heavy. I can't lift it."

Whereupon they both sat down and looked at the offending roll.

"I know," said Donny after a moment "I can pry it up and then you can slip that board under." He pointed to an old clapboard that had come loose from the hen house.

"Then what?" asked Linda.

"Then we'll pull the board and the wire to the edge of the bank and we'll put the cart down there and we'll push it over on it."

"Oh, boy! You're smart!" cried Linda, and she looked at her brother with pride, "and I'll hold it on the wagon while you pull it down to the sidewalk."

"I guess Daddy would call this using our heads," grunted Linda as she and Donny worked and struggled.

"I'm using more than that," muttered Donny as the sweat dripped off his face and he at last got the wire onto the cart.

At this point Eleanor came up, purring as if in praise. Slowly she led the way down the drive, the tip of her tail waving from side to side, her big feet crossing and recrossing in front of her.

When the children and Eleanor came puffing back up the drive with the empty wagon, Mrs. Bigelow came out to meet them. "Roast-beef sandwiches for two very good helpers," she beamed at them. "I went over to find you at the hen house and saw you had moved that big roll of wire all yourselves. Good for you!"

The children proudly told her how they had done it.

"He thought of the important part," admitted Linda, pointing to Donny. "I couldn't have figured that out."

"But you thought of the cart," Donny stated firmly. "I was going to try to do it with the wheelbarrow, which I can hardly lift anyway."

"It's nice working together, isn't it?" said Mrs. Bigelow, concealing her surprise at this new unity between her children.

"We really had three helpers, Mother," corrected Linda. "Eleanor came at the end and encouraged us. She should get a roast-beef sandwich, too."

"I'll make her a big one—without any bread," Mrs. Bigelow promised. And Eleanor, as if she understood, flashed her big yellow eyes at her mistress and slowly led the way to the kitchen door.

Word came that night that Gerty was fine but the veterinarian thought he ought to keep her four or five days so there would be no chance of infection.

Meanwhile the kittens thrived and played with each other constantly. When they went outside, they loved to hide from each other in some tall rhododendron plants in the front yard. Eleanor would stand guard and watch their antics with pride. But every once in a while she couldn't resist playing, too. As they tumbled over each other, she would bat them around, often not too gently. Or she would lie in the deep grass, just the tip of her tail twitching, waiting for them to come by, unsuspecting. Then she would leap out and they would all tussle. They had a wonderful time.

While Gerty was gone, Mrs. Bigelow tried to keep an eye on the cats when they were outdoors. But one day she was making a cake and ran out of sugar.

"I'm just going to the corner store for a moment," she called to the children. "Watch the cats. They are playing out in front."

But Donny was working on an airplane model upstairs in his room and Linda was washing her doll's hair at the kitchen sink. Their mother hadn't been gone but five minutes when a yowl came from the front yard followed by furious barking.

Donny threw his model on the bed, rushed down the stairs and outdoors. The two dogs who had led Gerty to her accident were in the yard, racing around a tree where Eleanor lay crouched on a limb. She was swelled up to twice her size and miaowing pitifully for help.

Just as Donny appeared, the police dog spied the kittens. They were huddled against the foundation of the house, too far from a tree to climb it even if they could. Howling, the big dog sprang across the yard toward them.

Donny, his eyes wide with horror, looked frantically for something to help defend the kittens. The old blanket he and his mother had used for Gerty still lay folded up on the back porch. He seized that and ran between them.

"Go away!" he cried, but the dog, angered at this obstruction, sprang at him, pulled the blanket from his grasp, knocking him to the ground. Donny tried to get up but the dog, snapping and snarling, would not let him.

Suddenly, Linda came bouncing out the back door. She was already screaming although no one had touched her. She started toward the kittens, but the big mongrel went for her and Linda kicked at him, meanwhile looking around wildly. Suddenly she spied the hose that lay coiled by an outside faucet near the back steps.

Her bellowing kept on and so did her kicks, but somehow she reached the faucet, which she turned on full blast. Then she grabbed the nozzle of the hose.

Rush came the water! Linda waved the nozzle around madly and at one point happened to direct it straight at the mongrel dog who was still snarling and jumping at her.

Smoosh! Right in the face she got him! He turned quickly around and made for the street while another wild sweep with the nozzle caught the police dog, who was still biting and snapping at Donny. First, the hard stream of water caught him in the tail. Then, as he wheeled around, it gushed full force into his eyes. Dazed, he shook his head, tucked his tail between his legs, tore up the drive, and out to the street.

There was a moment of complete silence except for the water gushing out of the nozzle now held upright so that it went all over Linda herself. She snorted, gulped, and wiped the water from her eyes with her skirt.

"Donny!" she cried, "Are you all right? What happened?"

"Yes, what on earth happened?" echoed Mrs. Bigelow, running up the drive, on edge with anxiety, having heard from afar the dogs' barking, Eleanor's howling, and Linda's screaming.

Donny struggled to his feet and started to explain.

"Those strange dogs got after Eleanor and me, and then Linda appeared. She saved the kittens and all of us by turning on the hose. Mother, she really *is* brave!"

Linda looked at her brother in astonishment. "I'm not. I really didn't dare do anything. It was Donny who was brave. He went right after the big dog who was going at the kittens. I grabbed the hose to keep the dogs off me, not to help anybody else."

"Oh, Linda!" cried Mrs. Bigelow, not knowing what story to believe.

"That's true, Mother," insisted Linda. "I wasn't brave a bit and now I know I never was. I just told the words. Donny is the brave one. And so is Eleanor and so is Gerty." At that she sat down hard on the back steps and burst into tears, her hands over her eyes.

"What's all this?" called a familiar voice, and a familiar booming bark sounded up the drive.

They all looked up to see Mr. Bigelow approaching with Gerty straining on a leash.

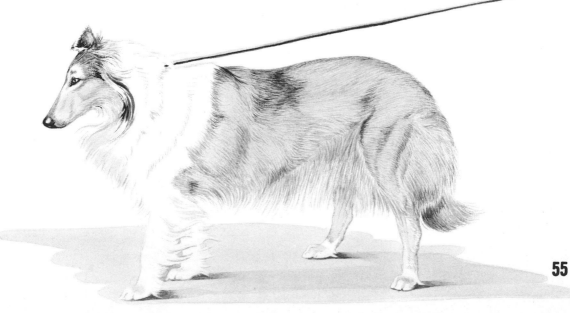

"We just had a dog-and-cat fight," explained Mrs. Bigelow as she bent down to unsnap Gerty's leash.

"And a dog-and-boy fight and a dog-and-girl fight," Linda continued. "It was war. It was awful!"

"I thought you liked war," her father teased.

"I don't any more," stated Linda flatly. "I'm going to be friends with everybody, even—"

"Me," added Donny, laughing. "Just like Gerty and Eleanor. Look!"

And, sure enough, there lay Gerty and Eleanor side by side on the driveway. Both seemed worn out but Gerty flopped her tail up and down a few times to show she heard. And Eleanor blinked her yellow eyes over the dog's head, as if to say, "That's right. We're friends."